Peli Can Surf

Written by Eric Noel Muñoz
Illustrated by Bonnie Bright

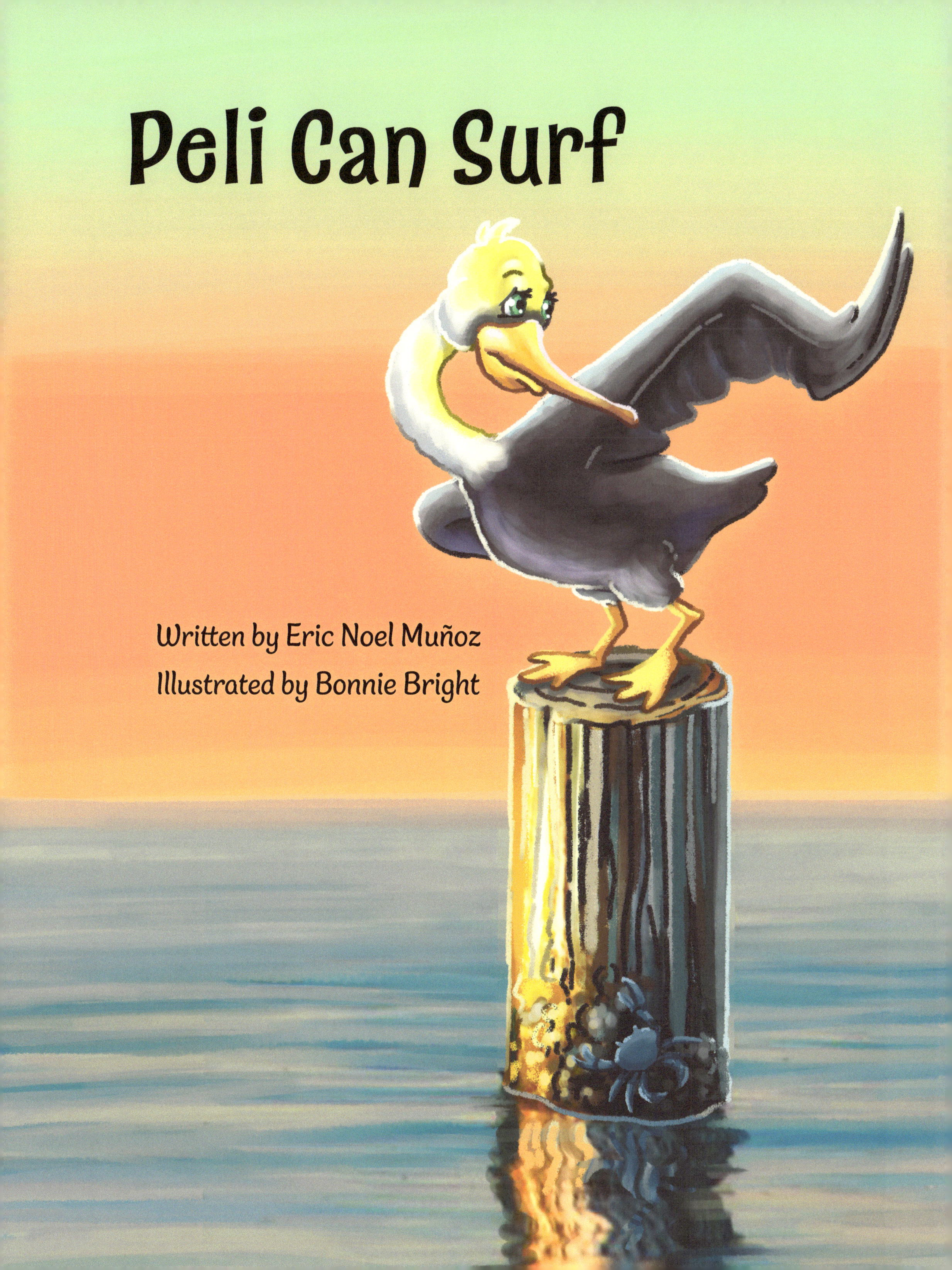

Peli Can Surf

Author, **Eric Noel Muñoz**
Illustrator, **Bonnie Bright**

ISBN 979-8-9916655-2-0

This Book Belongs To

____

Once, upon a beautiful coastline, a happy pelican named Peli was born to two parents who loved her very much.

Sadly, one of Peli's wings was different. The outer edge was turned upward on her left wing. However, her parents helped her learn to fly gracefully just like all of the other pelicans.

Peli loved watching how the grown-up pelicans flew together, in formation, as they rode the waves and glided over the ocean.

She dreamt of the day she would join them.

As Peli grew older, the other pelicans often made fun of her bent wing.

"Your parents named you Peli because you're only half a pelican!" They teased. They did not want her to fly in their formations. "You can't surf waves with a wing like that!" They said. Of course, Peli did not feel this way, and thought she could fly and surf just as well as the others.

So, Peli spent a lot time away from the other pelicans and found peace on isolated shorelines.

She learned to fly in light winds, and heavy winds. She learned to glide over large waves, and small waves.

And every night at sunset, she returned to her home lagoon, alone with her bent wing, while the other pelicans flew home together in formation.

One day, up the coast, the waves were smooth with good shape, and had beautiful, round, spitting tubes. Peli saw humans surfing with confidence and control as they entered and exited the tubes of the waves on their surfboards.

Peli studied how the humans rode the waves...

...how they slowed down by using their hand to let the wave surround them without losing too much speed.

“How exciting...I want to ride tubes like the humans.” Said Peli.

As Peli practiced, she soon realized that pressing her bent wing into the wave face could help her slow down so that the tube could surround her.

But this was very dangerous and she knew she had to practice her timing and surfing skills.

Peli went to sea caves and used her bent wing to catch the air when the water surged and gushed out. This was like the spit that would get blown out of a hollow wave.

Peli went to blowholes let the water spray her high up into the air. Her timing was getting very good.

Peli quickly learned how to use her bent wing...

...to ride the waves...

...and control her speed.

Soon she was able to surf the tubes, and used her skill and confidence to ride the round waves unlike any other pelican.

One day, she went back to where the humans were surfing, and they were amazed and impressed with her tube riding ability.

One surfer, known as Boss Jonny, paddled over to her and placed his necklace around her neck,

"Wow...you deserve this!" He said.

Peli felt honored to receive such praise.

But she always wished that her local crew of pelicans would accept her like the humans did. She watched them ride the waves together as they flew in a group formation.

One day, the waves at Peli's home beach got very large and tubular. All of the other pelicans sat safely on rocks or on the beach. They knew not to go near those gnarly and dangerous waves.

Except for Peli. She rode the tubes on those big, round waves using her bent wing. The other pelicans had never seen anything like it. Everyone saw how Peli's bent wing gave her control and allowed her to slow down so the huge wave could surround her.

On the largest wave of the day, Peli pulled into a huge, round tube and completely disappeared from view. The other pelicans were scared but many of them shouted,

"If anyone can, Peli can!"

...and then she came out of the tube with the spit gushing hard behind her! After that day, the pelicans wanted Peli to lead their flying formations and to ride the waves together. This made Peli very happy and her parents even more proud.

From that day forward, there were no pelicans left behind. To show respect to Peli, the other pelicans bent the tips of their wings while flying in formation.

And they would all shout out, “Peli Can Surf!”

Milton Keynes UK
Ingram Content Group UK Ltd.
UKHW050925121124
450964UK00010B/96